This book belongs to

_____

Adventures
iN Bikini Bottom

Stephen Hillenburg

Based on the TV series *SpongeBob SquarePants*® created by Steven Hillenburg
as seen on Nickelodeon®

SIMON SPOTLIGHT
An imprint of Simon & Schuster Children's Publishing Division
1230 Avenue of the Americas, New York, New York 10020
Camp SpongeBob and *Trouble at the Krusty Krab!* © 2004 Viacom International Inc.
UFO! © 2005 Viacom International Inc.
Hoedown Showdown © 2006 Viacom International Inc.
Manufactured in the United States of America
11 13 15 17 19 20 18 16 14 12
ISBN-13: 978-1-4169-1562-1
ISBN-10: 1-4169-1562-1
0312 LAK
These titles were previously published individually by Simon Spotlight.
These titles were previously catalogued individually by the Library of Congress.

Adventures
in Bikini Bottom

Ready-to-Read

Simon Spotlight/Nickelodeon

New York   London   Toronto   Sydney

Table of Contents

by Molly Reisner and Kim Ostrow
illustrated by Heather Martinez

It was a perfect summer day
in Bikini Bottom. Sandy spent
the morning practicing her new
karate moves.
"Hiiiyaaaa! All this sunshine
makes me more energetic
than a jackrabbit after a cup
of coffee," she said.

"Hey, Sandy, where did you first
learn karate anyway?"
SpongeBob asked.
Sandy told her friend about her days
at Master Kim's Karate Camp.

"... and I won the championship!"
Sandy finished breathlessly.
SpongeBob leaped in the air.
"Camp sounds amazing!" he shouted.
"But I never got to go."

"When I was little, my dream
   was to go to camp. But every summer
   my parents sent me to Grandma's.
   Sometimes I would pretend she was
   my counselor, but I am not sure she
   was cut out for camp life,"
   SpongeBob said, sighing.

"Say no more, SpongeBob,"
said Sandy. "Let's open Bikini
Bottom's first summer camp.
You can be my assistant."
"I can?" asked SpongeBob.
"Yes, and we can get started
today," said Sandy.
"I am ready!" shouted SpongeBob.

Sandy gathered Squidward and
Patrick to tell them about the camp.
"Oh, please," Squidward said,
moaning. "Camp is for children."
"Exactly!" shouted SpongeBob.
"It would be for all the little
children of Bikini Bottom."

"Hmmm," Squidward thought out loud. "Perhaps I could teach the kids around here a thing or two. Everyone would look up to me."

"That sounds like lots of fun,"
said Patrick. "When I was at starfish
camp, we used to lie around in the sun
and sleep a lot. I could teach
everyone how to do that!"

"I will teach karate!"
declared Sandy, kicking the air.

"Now go on home and practice what you are going to teach. Let's meet back here tomorrow," said Sandy.

The next day SpongeBob woke up
in the best mood ever.
"To be a good assistant, I need
to make sure I am prepared
with good camper activities,"
he told Gary.
SpongeBob thought of making Krabby
Patties and having bubble-blowing
contests. He imagined whole days
spent jellyfishing.

SpongeBob ran around his house
gathering all the items he needed.
"Whistle! Check. Megaphone! Check.
Visor! Check. Clipboard?"
Gary slithered over
to SpongeBob's bed and meowed.
"Good job, Gary! Check!"

SpongeBob went over to the mirror
and raised his arms. "Camping
assistants need to be strong!"
he reminded himself
as he flexed his muscles.
"Now I am ready!"

SpongeBob ran over
to the treedome.
Sandy was chopping
wood with her bare hands.
"SpongeBob SquarePants reporting
for duty!" he said, blowing his
whistle three times.

"As a good assistant, I request permission to check on everyone to make sure they are practicing their duties."

"Go for it, SpongeBob," said Sandy.

First SpongeBob went to Patrick's
rock. He watched quietly as Patrick
practiced the art of sleeping.
Then SpongeBob blew his whistle.
Patrick jumped up.
"Just making sure you are working
  hard," explained SpongeBob.
"Now go back to sleep!"

Next SpongeBob peeked
inside Squidward's house.
"I can't hear you," sang SpongeBob.
"Practice makes perfect."

SpongeBob went back to see Sandy,
who was working on her karate moves.
"All counselors are working hard,"
reported SpongeBob.
"Now what should I do?"

"Take a load off and have some
   lemonade," suggested Sandy.
"No time for lemonade,"
   said SpongeBob. "As your assistant,
I am here to assist.
How can I assist?"

"Listen, little buddy," said Sandy.
"You are acting nuttier than a bag
of walnuts at the county fair.
This camp is supposed to be fun."
"I will make sure it is fun!
With my assistance, this will be
the best camp ever!" SpongeBob said,
cheering.

"Attention, counselors, please
report to me right away,"
SpongeBob said. They all ran to him.
"Now go back to your posts and
PRACTICE! Camp opens tomorrow."

That night SpongeBob was so
excited, he could not sleep.
He decided to visit all
the counselors just to make sure
they were ready.

"Squidward," he whispered.
Squidward was fast asleep.
SpongeBob blew his whistle.
"Just making sure you are all
set for tomorrow."
"You are killing me, SpongeBob,"
said Squidward, and he went
back to sleep.

The next morning a very annoyed
Squidward and sleepy Patrick
headed over to Sandy's treedome.
"What are we going to do about
SpongeBob?" asked Squidward.
"I refuse to be ordered around
by him anymore."

"I have just the thing
for the little guy," said Sandy.

"To express our gratitude
for all your hard work, we have a
small present for you," said Sandy.
"For me?" asked SpongeBob.
SpongeBob opened the box.
Inside was a camp uniform.

"We would like you to be the very
first camper," said Sandy.
"But don't you need me to work?"
asked SpongeBob.
"Nope. We were all so busy preparing
for camp that we never advertised
for campers! You are our first
and only camper!" exclaimed Sandy.

SpongeBob put on his uniform.
"SpongeBob SquarePants
reporting to camp!" he shouted,
running to his counselors.
"I am ready!"

TROUBLE AT THE KRUSTY KRAB!

adapted by Steven Banks
illustrated by Zina Saunders
based on the movie written by Derek Drymon,
Tim Hill, Steve Hillenburg, Kent Osborne,
Aaron Springer, and Paul Tibbitt

There was trouble
at the Krusty Krab!
Police helicopters
circled above town.
The people of Bikini Bottom
had gathered to see
what was going on.

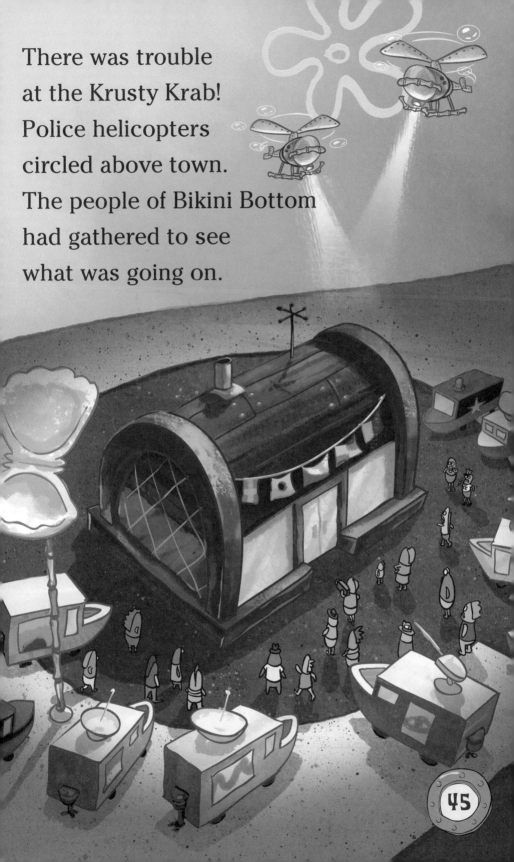

News reporters came up to
the owner, Mr. Krabs.
"The people want to know:
What is going on?"
asked a reporter.

"Settle down! Please!"
shouted Mr. Krabs.
"We have a problem here
that I would rather not discuss
until my manager gets here!"

47

Just then a car pulled up,
and out stepped
SpongeBob SquarePants.
The crowd cheered!

"My manager is here!"
cried Mr. Krabs with a sigh
of relief. "The day is saved!
He will know what to do!"

"Talk to me, Krabs,"
said SpongeBob.
"It started out as a simple order:
a Krabby Patty with cheese,"
said Mr. Krabs.

"So what went wrong?"
asked SpongeBob.
"The customer took a bite
and . . . and . . . and . . ."
Mr. Krabs couldn't go on.

"Spit it out, Krabs!"
cried SpongeBob.
"THERE WAS NO CHEESE!"
shouted Mr. Krabs
as he started to cry.
"Get a hold of yourself, Eugene,"
cried SpongeBob.

53

SpongeBob faced the crowd.
"Okay, everyone," said SpongeBob,
"I am going in."
Patrick ran up to SpongeBob
and begged, "Do not do it!
It's too dangerous!"
SpongeBob smiled. "Do not worry.
'Dangerous' is my middle name!"

As SpongeBob walked up
to the door he said,
"If I do not make it back alive,
give all my jellyfishing nets
to Squidward."
"I do not want them!"
yelled Squidward from the crowd.

The crowd watched as SpongeBob
entered the Krusty Krab.
"Will SpongeBob be able to get
some cheese on that patty,
Mr. Krabs?" asked a reporter.

"He has to! He must!" said Mr. Krabs.
"But what if he can't?"
asked the reporter.
"THEN THE WORLD AS WE KNOW IT
IS OVER!" cried Mr. Krabs.

The customer who had
ordered the Krabby Patty sat
in the corner of the restaurant.
He looked up at SpongeBob.
"Who are you?" he asked.
"I am the manager of this place,"
said SpongeBob.

"I am really scared, man!"
cried the customer.
SpongeBob replied, "Do not worry.
Everything is going to be fine."

Outside, the crowd waited.
A reporter spoke into a microphone
saying, "SpongeBob has been
inside for ten seconds!"
"The suspense is killing me!"
cried Mr. Krabs.
"Me too," said Patrick,
eating an ice-cream cone.

Back inside, SpongeBob sat down with the customer. "Do you have a name?" asked SpongeBob.

"My name is Phil," said the customer.

SpongeBob nodded and said, "That's a good name."

"YOU DO NOT UNDERSTAND!"
screamed Phil.
"I CANNOT TAKE IT! THERE WAS
NO CHEESE!"

"Stay with me, Phil!"
said SpongeBob.
"Do you have a family?"
"Yes," replied Phil.
"I have a lovely wife
and two great children."
"That's what it is all about,"
said SpongeBob.

"Okay, Phil," said SpongeBob.
"Stay calm. I am just going to
 open my briefcase."
"Why?" cried Phil.
"I have only got one shot at this,
 and I have to get out the
 right tools for the job,"
 said SpongeBob.

SpongeBob reached into the
briefcase and pulled out a pair of
solid gold tweezers.
"Solid gold tweezers!" shouted Phil.
"Yes, they are!"
said SpongeBob.

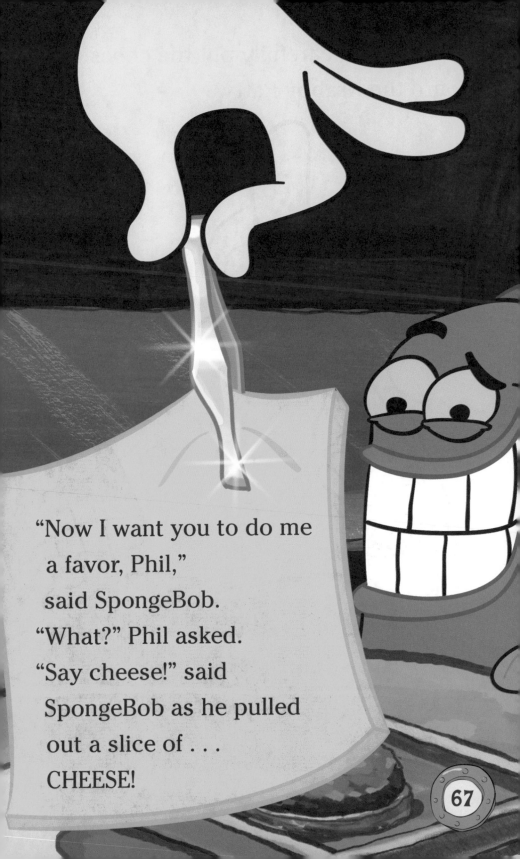

"Now I want you to do me
  a favor, Phil,"
said SpongeBob.
"What?" Phil asked.
"Say cheese!" said
  SpongeBob as he pulled
  out a slice of . . .
CHEESE!

SpongeBob carefully put the cheese onto the Krabby Patty.

Success! The cheese was on
the Krabby Patty!
SpongeBob marched out of the
Krusty Krab with a smiling Phil
by his side.
"Order up!" cried SpongeBob.

"SpongeBob, I would like to give you the Manager of the Year Award!" said Mr. Krabs. SpongeBob just smiled back, looking pleased with himself.

Then Mr. Krabs turned to Phil and said, "And that will be two dollars and ninety-five cents for the Krabby Patty, Phil."

Suddenly the crowd gathered around
SpongeBob and lifted him up
in the air.
"Three cheers for the manager!"
cried Mr. Krabs. "Hip hip!"
Honk!
"Hip, hip!" shouted Mr. Krabs.
Honk!

Honk!

Honk!

Honk!

"What's that noise?"
wondered SpongeBob.

"Sounds like an alarm clock
going off to me," said Patrick.

"It's my alarm clock!"
said SpongeBob.

"I must be dreaming!"

Honk!

SpongeBob woke up in his bed.
"Gary, I had my favorite
dream again about being the manager
of the Krusty Krab! Do you think it
will ever happen, Gary?"
"Meow," said Gary.
SpongeBob smiled.
"That is exactly how I feel!"

by Adam Beechen
illustrated by Zina Saunders

"Grow, flower, grow!
Grow, flower, grow!"
SpongeBob and his best friend,
Patrick, sang as they marched
through SpongeBob's garden.

"What are you two
weirdos doing?"
Squidward asked.

"If you talk to plants,
    they grow fast," Patrick told him.
"And if we sing to my daffodils,
    they should grow even faster!"
    SpongeBob added.

Squidward was about to tell them
to be quiet, when suddenly . . .

something very big blocked
out the light from above!

83

Everyone in Bikini Bottom met
to talk about what had happened.
They decided aliens must be
invading Bikini Bottom.

"We should run and hide!"
someone shouted.
"No, we should hide and then run!"
someone shouted back.

Patrick got scared and ran around in circles.
"I do not know whether to run or hide!" he cried.

Squidward headed to his house.
"I do not think it's the
end of the world," he grumbled.
"Everyone should go home and stop
making so much noise!"

"Maybe this is not the end
of the world," Sandy suggested.
"Maybe it's just something we do
not understand yet."

"If Sandy is not scared,
then neither am I,"
SpongeBob said.

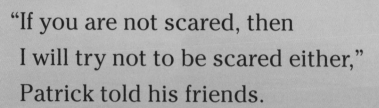

"If you are not scared, then
    I will try not to be scared either,"
    Patrick told his friends.
"Well, we are scared,"
    everyone else said.
"And we are going to
    run and hide!"

"What are we going to do?"
SpongeBob asked.
"I think we should find out
what is making that shadow,"
Sandy told him.

THIS MIGHT
BE IT!!!

SALE!

"We can use my rocket ship
to take us to the Outer Waters
so we can get a closer look,"
Sandy said.

The friends gathered everything
they would need for their trip.
"Why do we need sandwiches?"
Sandy asked Patrick.
"Rockets make me hungry,"
Patrick explained.

They climbed into the rocket ship.
"Buckle up, fellas. It is going
to be a bumpy ride!" Sandy shouted
as they blasted off.

Patrick buckled in his sandwiches.

95

They saw all sorts of creatures
they had never seen before.
Patrick was a little scared,
but he tried to be brave
like SpongeBob and Sandy.

Back in his house in Bikini Bottom,
Squidward suddenly realized
how quiet it was outside.
He had not been scared of the
shadow before, but he was now.

Suddenly there was a loud knock
at his door!
"Squidward!" Mrs. Puff shouted
from the other side of the door.
"Are you sure you do not want
to come hide with us?"

"No," Squidward yelled back.
"I am not scared! I am busy playing
my clarinet!"
He tried to play his clarinet,
but he was so scared, it sounded
even worse than usual!

When Mrs. Puff and Mr. Krabs left,
Squidward quickly hid under his bed.
"I am not letting the end of the world
get me . . . or my clarinet!" he said.

Sandy's rocket soared closer
and closer to the shadow.
Patrick became more and more scared.
He could not help it.

"What if that shadow really is the end of the world?" Patrick asked. "Then at least we will have seen it up close," SpongeBob answered. "And we will have seen it together," Sandy agreed.

Finally, they were close enough
to see what was making the shadow—
and they could not believe it!

"Hey, guys," said their old friend
  Stan the manta.
"I am back from school
  to visit Bikini Bottom!"
"Wow! You got big," Sandy gasped.

"Why are you up here blocking all
the light?" Sandy asked. "You really
spooked everybody!"
"I am sorry," Stan told them.
"I could not remember
where I used to live."

"We will show you the way,"
SpongeBob said.
"Everyone will be happy to see you!"
"Especially since you are not
the end of the world," Patrick said.
No one was happier than he was!

Everyone was very happy to see Stan
again. They celebrated by playing
a new game Patrick made up called
run-and-hide-and-seek.

Squidward did not play along.
If he had played, he would have won.
He stayed in his hiding place
for two weeks!

by Kelli Chipponeri
illustrated by Vince DePorter

SpongeBob and Patrick were excited.
The Bikini Bottom Rodeo was tonight!

"I am excited to be in the
sea horse rodeo," said SpongeBob.

"I can't wait to ride the giant clam!" Patrick said.

"Are you ready to do the square-dance calls for the hoedown?" asked Patrick.

"Of course," replied SpongeBob.
But he really wasn't—he had
forgotten that he was the caller!
"Uh, Patrick, maybe we should
get ready," said SpongeBob.

After they got dressed, SpongeBob
and Patrick were all set to go.

SpongeBob and Patrick arrived
at the rodeo. First they went to
the sea horse corral. SpongeBob
showed off his skills on the sea horse
and came in third place!

Then they stopped by the
giant clam.
At first Patrick held on tight.

But then he let go to fix his hat—
and fell off the clam!

Finally they went to
the square-dance tent
for the hoedown.
"Hi, boys!" called Sandy Cheeks.
"SpongeBob, are you ready to be
the square-dance caller?"

"Ready? Uh, yes, I'm ready!" said SpongeBob. "I can hardly wait," said Squidward.

SpongeBob went up to the mike.
"Uh, ahem. Well, I guess I should
get started," he said.
"Please find a partner."

The Bikini Bottom Uptown
Hoedown Band began to play.
SpongeBob looked at the dancers.
Everyone looked back at him.
SpongeBob cleared his throat.
He didn't know what to say next.

Then he remembered something
he had seen on TV a long time ago.
"Swing your partner to and fro,"
SpongeBob called. "Step to the right
and away we go!"

To his surprise, the dancers did what he said! They held hands and skipped in a circle until they came back to where they had started.

"Now do what?" SpongeBob wondered
out loud.
The dancers thought he called,
"Now doughnut!"

Not sure what to do,
they all skipped over to
the snack table.
The dancers crashed into one another
as they reached for the doughnuts.

"No, come back!" yelled SpongeBob. But the dancers heard, "Now, kick back!"

The dancers looked at one another and kicked their legs backward.

"Hey, watch out," yelled Squidward as Patrick kicked him.

Mr. Krabs lost his balance.
Sandy tried to help but
got pinched by Mr. Krabs's claws.
"Ouch!" cried Sandy.

"Stop! Stop!" SpongeBob yelled.
But the dancers heard, "Chop-chop!"
They started chopping at one another.

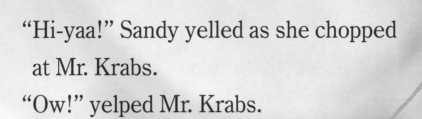

"Hi-yaa!" Sandy yelled as she chopped at Mr. Krabs.

"Ow!" yelped Mr. Krabs.

SpongeBob was about to give up.
Everyone was fighting instead of
dancing!

Then SpongeBob had an idea.

He grabbed a doughnut

and walked over to the dancers.

"Stop, everyone!" he called out.

He took a deep breath.

"Just follow me," he said.

"Here's the doughnut.

"This is how you kick back.

"And here's how you chop-chop!"

"Now, are you ready?" asked SpongeBob.
"Ready!" replied the dancers.

SpongeBob started calling,

"Swing your partner to and fro.

Step to the right and away we go!"

"Now, doughnut!" he called.
The group held hands and
began shuffling in a circle
to the right.

SpongeBob was happy.
He was calling a square dance!

"That was pretty fancy calling!"
   said Sandy.
"You could say I learned on my feet,"
   SpongeBob said.
"So let's do another dance—
   with new moves!" said Sandy.